HEALTH HARRY'S
ALKALINE FRUIT ADVENTURE

WHERE IS THE SQUARE?

story **GLESTER THORPE**
art **JOHN MAHOMET**

"HEY KIDS, I'M HEALTHY HARRY. WHAT ARE YOUR NAMES?"

"I'M PAM."   "I'M LARRY."   "I'M SUE."   "I'M JAMES."

**"I HAVE A SECRET. WOULD YOU LIKE TO HEAR?"
THE KIDS YELLED OUT, "YEAH!"**

"TO GROW HEALTHY AND STRONG
AND TO KEEP SICKNESS AWAY,
YOU MUST EAT FIVE ALKALINE FRUITS A DAY."

"KIDS! LOOK THIS WAY!
GO OUT AND GET THESE FIVE ALKALINE FRUITS TODAY:
APPLES, PLUMS, PEACHES, CHERRIES AND PEARS.
YOU CAN FIND THEM AT A PLACE NAMED THE SQUARE.

COME BACK TOMORROW AFTER YOUR FEAST.
THEN I'LL GIVE YOU FIVE MORE ALKALINE FRUITS TO EAT."

"HEY THERE KIDS!. I'M LEE THE BEE!
WHY ARE YOU WALKING ON MY STREET?"
"WE'RE LOOKING FOR APPLES, PLUMS, PEACHES, CHERRIES AND PEARS.
HEALTHY HARRY SAID WE COULD FIND THEM AT THE SQUARE."

"IF YOU WALK DOWN THE ROAD, YOU'LL SEE A RAT NAMED PAT.
HE SHOULD BE ABLE TO HELP YOU WITH THAT."

"HELLO. ARE YOU PAT THE RAT?
DO YOU KNOW WHERE THE SQUARE IS AT?"
" YES, I'M THE RAT NAMED PAT.
THE SQUARE, WHY DO YOU ASK ME THAT?"

"WE'RE LOOKING FOR APPLES, PLUMS, PEACHES, CHERRIES AND PEARS. HEALTHY HARRY SAID WE COULD FIND THEM AT THE SQUARE."
" I'M NOT SURE. COME INTO MY HOUSE. ASK MY SON. HE'S THE LITTLE MOUSE."

"HI LITTLE MOUSE. COULD YOU HELP US OUT?"
"YES, BUT WHAT ARE YOU TALKING ABOUT?"

"DO YOU KNOW WHICH WAY IS THE SQUARE?"
THE MOUSE SAID, "GO UP THE HILL AND ASK THE MEAN BEAR."

PAM LOOKED BACK AND MADE A FUSS, THEN ASKED, "WHAT IS THAT UGLY THING FOLLOWING US?"

"MY NAME IS SICKNESS, HOW ARE YOU?
IF YOU DON'T EAT FIVE ALKALINE FRUITS TODAY, I'LL GET YOU!
WHEN I GET YOU, YOU WON'T LIKE IT ONE BIT
BECAUSE ALL OF YOU WILL SURELY BECOME SICK."

SUE YELLED OUT, "LET'S MOVE ON."

"I DON'T WANT TO GET SICK.
I WANT TO BE HEALTHY AND STRONG!"

THE MEAN BEAR SWUNG HIS PAW AND ASKED, "WHO GOES THERE?"
LARRY SAID, " WE'RE JUST TRYING TO FIND THE SQUARE."

"SORRY KIDS I DIDN'T SEE YOU.
OKAY, LET ME TELL YOU WHAT TO DO.
KEEP WALKING AND YOU'LL SEE A SNAKE.
HE'LL KNOW WHERE TO GO. HIS NAME IS JAKE."

"HELLO, ARE YOU JAKE THE SNAKE?"
"YES, BUT I'M BARELY AWAKE."

"ANY QUESTIONS YOU HAVE, YOU'LL HAVE TO ASK THE SNAIL. SHE'S VERY NICE. HER NAME IS MEL."

"OH, NO! SICKNESS IS BACK."
"LET'S RUN BEFORE HE ATTACKS."

"YES, I'M BACK AND I'M GETTING CLOSE.
DO YOU WANT TO BE SICK? I'LL GIVE YOU A DOSE."

"HOW ARE YOU, MEL THE SNAIL?"
"I'M GREAT AND DOING SWELL."
"COULD YOU KINDLY TELL US HOW TO GET TO THE SQUARE?
IT'S THE PLACE WITH APPLES, PLUMS, PEACHES, CHERRIES AND PEARS?"

"GO AROUND THE CORNER. YOU'RE DOING SO WELL.
ASK THE SKUNK WITH THE STINKY SMELL."

"HELLO KIDS. WHAT'S GOING ON?"
LARRY SAID, "WE'RE TRYING TO BECOME HEALTHY AND STRONG."

"THAT MEANS YOU MUST BE HEADED TO THE SQUARE.
THE BIRD HAS GREAT EYES.
HE'LL SHOW YOU HOW TO REACH THERE."

"HELLO MR. BIRD. IS THE SQUARE CLOSE?"

"YES! GO TALK TO THE MAN STANDING NEXT TO THE POST."

"HELLO KIDS. WELCOME TO THE SQUARE.
SICKNESS CANNOT CATCH YOU IN HERE.
GO RIGHT IN AND HAVE A FEAST.
GET THE ALKALINE FRUITS YOU WERE SENT HERE TO EAT."

"HEALTHY HARRY WAS RIGHT! THERE'S ALKALINE FRUIT EVERYWHERE! THERE ARE APPLES, PEACHES, PLUMS, CHERRIES AND PEARS!"

"NOW THAT WE'VE HAD FIVE ALKALINE FRUITS TODAY, WE CAN GROW HEALTHY AND STRONG AND KEEP SICKNESS AWAY!"

"LET'S GET BACK TO HEALTHY HARRY!"

Made in United States
Orlando, FL
04 December 2022